More of

Betty the Fairytale Detective

By

Spike Brown

Illustrations by Sharon Maynard Burrows

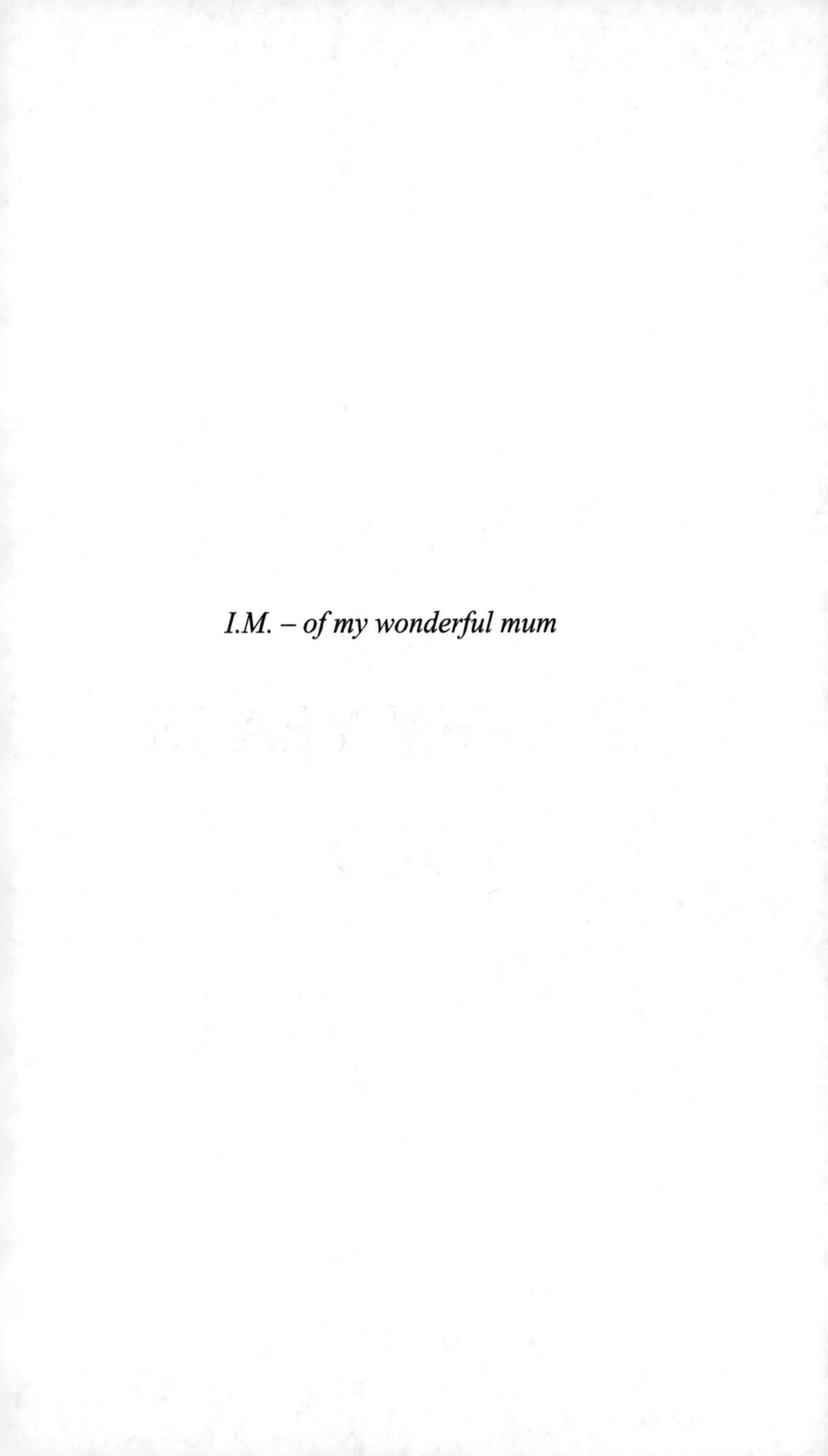

I.M. – of my wonderful mum

ELEVEN YEARS

OLD

CHAPTER

L arna Amberley sat in her wheeled invalid chair, her foot encased in plaster, gazing wistfully out of the mullioned window of Mulberry Manor – her home, watching the snow fall. She was a bit peeved because the violin she used for her music lessons had gone missing. Plonking about on crutches she was with the teacher for over two hours that afternoon in the sitting room.

A servant, Mr Evans, entered, placing another log on the fire. Larna's fingers gripped the armrest fiercely.

"Evans, be so good as to take me to my grandmother in five minutes, will you?"

"Very well, Miss Larna."

"Any news of my violin?"

"I'm afraid not, ma'am."

When he had left, a fiery log shifted in the grate causing a flurry of sparks to rise up the chimney. The hands on the ormolu clock on the mantelpiece started to spin backwards.

"Stop it, Tudor," Miss Amberley said curtly. "You're to stop that, y'hear? None of your nonsense. I mean it."

No one else was in the room, her outburst only witnessed by a garden sparrow as it fluttered onto the stone windowsill, peering through the pane inquisitively.

Clever Betty, her friend, had been invited to stay the weekend – maybe she could fathom the instruments sudden disappearance.

That evening, the girls hurried down the end of the manor house gardens - the lit circle from the lens of a tiny brass lamp bobbed about along the frosty path. Larna's chair on wheels creaking forwards, her weighty plaster leg stuck straight out.

"Hmmm," said Zmunxy, musing on the problem, "I'll find that violin, can't be far away."

"Thanks awfully, Betty, but great crackerjack, I must introduce... oh you don't know Tudor do you? She's dying to meet you, honestly."

The lamplight struck an ivy-clad mausoleum. A carved stone tablet sent a chill down Betty's spine.

Tudor Sefton

died of typhus
that plagued Mulberry hamlet.
A contagion that took many
of the young in the year 1603
to their maker.

Beloved daughter of
the Lord of the manor
Sir Fitzroy Sefton

Without warning, the metal frame of the iron bars protecting the vault's entrance raised like a portcullis, the nail-studded door creaked open.

Taking the hint, Betty bumped her friend's wheelchair up the stone step. They found themselves inside a gloomy chamber. An effervescence of weird, floating green bubbles spread illumination. A slim, pale ghost girl appeared wearing a gown, her long, colour streaked hair parted, her sharp nose and chin jutting with determination. Tudor pointed at the cobwebby ceiling of the vault and smiled. How far removed from a perceived spectral encounter could you get?

She worked a lever and the roof of the vault unbelievably, slid back – stone grating against stone – allowing a glimpse of the night sky. After this incredible turn, even more surprisingly, a coffin decked with a lantern jerked up from its plinth, hovering in mid-air.

Betty realised what Larna Amberley already knew. The flying coffin was for real! The lamp on a stick sort of winked its light a couple of times. Tudor hopped in, and with the use of a paddle to steer, to manoeuvre, the coffin rose through the gap in the roof, rotated then – quickly attaining flight – whizzed around the manor garden a couple of times, flying above the glasshouses, before turning back and re-entering the old vault, landing perfectly level.

"That looks like fun," Betty had to admit. "Sort of outdoors pursuits."

The coffin pilot nodded, stowing her nifty paddle, knowing she was understood. Reaching over her knees to retract a lever, the coffin clunked down on the granite plinth carved with cherubic angels at each corner. Jumping out, she shooed them away. "Be seeing ya! Found that violin yet, Larna?"

That night, Betty shared a bedroom with Larna. For now, the priority for her was that violin. She was convinced it may have been worth a lot – stolen from Larna Amberley, right under her nose. She must be on the watch – the alert – for any possible leads amongst those who staffed Mulberry Manor, who worked for the ultra-stern grandmother.

Snow started falling again at around midnight —
the girls were both sound asleep. Betty awoke,
becoming aware of a tap-tapping on the glass of the
latticed window. She got out of bed and, bare-
footed, softly pattered over to draw the curtains
back.

Tap-tap-tap-tap.

"Alright, alright," she whispered, trying not to
wake Larna.

Betty peered outside at the dark, her bleary eyes

taking some time to adjust after being woken up. Finally, she could see a familiar skinny, sharp-featured girl with long, centre-parted hair dyed mauve and streaked with yellow. Betty had never seen this stark, bright colouration of hair before on girls. The phantom greeted the bed-riser.

"Hi, it's me, Tudor Sefton. Open the window and climb out. It's OK, you'll be safe."

"Climb into what?" Betty asked, feeling a little nervous.

Betty couldn't believe what was being asked of her. The flying coffin with its lantern on a stick hovered two storeys up, flush against the stone ledge of the house. It seemed an awful long way down from the eaves if you slipped. Might she be dreaming, though? Her fears seemed to subside, freeing her from acting scared.

The pale-faced spirit girl, with her angular cheeks and pointy nose, looked insulted. "Sorry, Tudor," the schoolgirl apologised. "Just let me fetch my silk slippers and dressing gown. I've just gotten up."

Larna's eiderdown was drawn almost over her head, her tufty hair unbothered by the wide-open window and freezing draught. Neither was she disturbed by her sharer beetling about the room searching for her dressing gown. Both the minute and hour hands of the alarm clock on the bedside cabinet eerily stopped at two in the morning.

Finally locating her stray slipper, hurriedly pulling it onto her cold foot, the junior sleuth was ready to go.

"Are you sure? Really one hundred-per-cent sure the coffin is strong enough for the pair of us, Tudor?"

"Course it is, Betty," the ghost girl answered. "They built 'em reinforced in the olden times. Plenty of nails and lead. You'll love it. Here, grab a paddle. You won't fall through, I promise. Aren't the brass handles nice and shiny?"

Stepping onto a wooden toy box, Betty managed to clamber onto the windowsill manoeuvring herself across the narrow gap, holding onto the outstretched paddle, at first faltering, swaying slowly, praying the screws would hold and not ping out one by one.

Showing oodles of confidence, Tudor Sefton sat in the front of her outlandish craft. The glowing lantern on a stick acted as a heater, casting a band of warmth around the dimensions of the coffin, this despite the freezing weather, the fact it was snowing, flakes the size of tiny feathers.

After a shaky start, Zmunxy clambered aboard, lowering herself down, much like climbing into a kayak, or canoe. Quite comfortable with the paddle, the shifting of weight seemed to make little difference

No sooner were both girls positioned than the extraordinary coffin tilted to the right, skated across the chimney tops before whizzing off in a curve round the garden. Tudor's long, streaky hair flowing back over her turned up collar. Betty had to admit the ride was fun, the view sensational.

"Paddle to the left, you nit wit, the left. It's all about intuition ..."

"Where are we headed, if you don't mind me asking?"

"To find the missing violin. You see, it's very

valuable. It's a genuine Stradivarius. The silly old bat of a grandma just has no idea. She couldn't have cared less when she found it up in the attic and started Larna on her music lessons. A violin is just a violin to her, but Evans, the butler, saw something. His eyes must have popped out on stalks.

The butler lived at a cottage in the grounds so by peeking in at the open mouthed, snoring Mr Evans second floor bedroom window there was spied the violin leaning up against his wardrobe – *flying coffins definitely have their uses.*

Tudor manoeuvred her weird kayak closer to the cottage sill – Betty prised open the rotten window frame, jumped into the room and retrieved the valuable Stradivarius, leaving the violin case as plain evidence. Evans none the wiser. Now that's what you call clever sleuthing. Larna imitating her haughty grandmother's voice to a tee, phoned Wellingford police and a dawn raid ensued.

"I am very impressed by Betty," Larna told her Grandmother later, after the police had gone.

"Well, I'm not. Catching crooks? So unladylike. That's a man's occupation, surely. Getting you to impersonate me on the phone, indeed. Is this Tudor Sefton's influence? I think it must be. That dratted ghost. Why doesn't she stay put in her vault."

CHAPTER

2

Message

The first occasion Betty Zmunx actually ever talked with Flo Dainty, a long-time resident of Glim Glumswick village, occupying one of the Georgian- style houses on the green, was at the beginning of May, along the High Street. Then, she seemed very cheerful and friendly.

What happened was this. Flo's partner, her housekeeper and companion, Miss Shelley, popped into the post office for stamps, leaving Miss Dainty stood outside studying the notices. Accidentally, she dropped her leather handbag, spilling out her purse, powder compact, and odds and ends onto the pavement. Betty and Winnie White, being nearby, coming out of Mrs Staple's sweet shop, rushed to her aid, gathering up the scattered items, returning the handbag to its rightful owner.

Visiting her local library in June, Betty was shocked to see Miss Cooter, the junior, hurrying over to assist Flo Dainty, who had just fallen out of a bath chair, collapsing in a tangled, knotted heap of tartan rug, helpless and seemingly unconscious. Her companion, Miss Shelley, an enormously broad-shouldered, squat lady in tweeds, protested.

"I can manage, thank you, dear. Flo *will* have her fits at the most inconvenient times. She *will*, however, recover. I shall apply smelling salts thus – voilà! Are you alright now?" There was a bitterness to her shrill voice. "How many times have I warned you about that sweet tooth, Flo? I ask you!" She glanced at Betty, seeming to sneer. "Honestly, her childish demands for third helpings of sticky toffee pudding and sherry trifle."

"A doctor might be able to advise," suggested the junior librarian. "Revise her dietary requirements, I mean." Miss Cooter's attention was, for a time, wholly taken up by a smart young man who had bounded into the library wearing a snazzy grey morning suit and bowler.

Betty recognised him as the apprentice draughtsman at Stanley's architect's office who sung in the choir.

About to return to her desk, Miss Cooter added, "Flo does look a bit *under the weather*, Miss Shelley."

"Should be fit as a fiddle if I had my way. All put on to gain attention, isn't it, Flo? You *will* have to lose weight, darling. I'm not going to keep lifting you up like this."

Eyes fluttered, Flo Dainty herself was hauled back into a sitting position, she could barely remain upright, drooling down her chin. She tried to utter something barely intelligible but failed. "Flo must simply learn to do without, then we avoid *silly fits* promoted by her wilful, selfish disobedience of my wishes."

Betty thought Miss Shelley insensitive and horrid. This moment of genuine sympathy for a person now confined to a bath chair, pushed about by a domineering, stronger partner must have conveyed itself upon the sufferer, for Flo Dainty distinctly formed a smile and, unnoticed by Miss Shelley, managed to press a library book into Betty's hands, tapping her hooked, beaky nose with a faltering finger as if to imply 'I'm sure you can keep a confidence, my dear'. The lady in her wheelchair and the carer, departed the library soon after.

The book was a Jane Austen novel; the girl supposed the Brontës, Charles Dickens and Trollope were Miss Dainty's preferred authors. She sat down at a little table in the reading section, spreading the first pages open upon her knee.

A thin piece of paper fluttered out, folded over once. Bits of paper, cigarette cards used as makeshift bookmarks, were common enough left behind by a

previous reader. She snatched it up and was appalled to read: *Help me, I am being murdered. F.D.* This written in a shaky hand with a blotchy nib in green ink.

Betty was distracted by the library cart rumbling along the parquet floor on its castors. Glancing up, she saw pretty Miss Cooter, the junior, pausing to replace a pile of recently returned books along the shelf.

On the spur of the moment, she stepped over to the cart and asked gaily, "Bet you that those Jane Austen and Brontë novels were loaned by Flo Dainty. Am I right?"

"Spot on, Betty," replied Miss Cooter with a grin. "She likes Anthony Trollope and the *Barchester*

Chronicles, Dickens, that sort of thing."

"And her companion, Miss Shelley? Romance, pot boilers?"

"No, illustrated cookbooks, nature and horticulture, biographies; non-fiction is more her line. Miss Shelley's 'returns' are on the trolley."

Betty Zmunx sidled up to the library cart, briefly scanning the glossy covers. Certain of the titles caused her concern, to inwardly question, prompting her to wonder seriously if she had better contact P.C. Johns at the police house. But were the titles, the subject matter, certain of Miss Shelley's returned books, merely coincidental? Was she making erroneous conclusions? No time like the present. If the message was genuine, a plea for help, something should be done, and done quickly. Betty decided to gather her best friends, Lizzie Meredith and Winnie White, and take practical steps.

Using the public footpath behind Flo Dainty's

Georgian property facing onto the green to reach the woods behind, the gang of girls scrambled upwards, plodding through the foliage and branches, the tangle of bracken.

"So many mushrooms growing up here on the woodland floor, just look at these!" cried Winnie White excitedly. "Ugly living growths of spongy fungi sprouting from tree roots. Even if it's edible I should hate it."

"Toadstools, big and small, the woodland dell's full of them. What time did you say horrid Miss Shelley takes her afternoon stroll, Betty?" queried Lizzie.

"Half past one on the dot. I think I can see her leaving the back door. Gracious, we had better hide in those bushes when she walks past. As I said, all of us must hurry back down to the green if my idea is to work."

"A jolly clever idea," admitted Lizzie, full of

admiration, kneeling down beside her best friend. "Gosh, straight out of a girl's adventure annual."

A bushy-tailed grey squirrel scuttled up the side of a tree trunk and, as superior as could be, gazed down at them from a branch, munching on a fir cone. A clatter of beating wings announced a pair of magpies.

Undergrowth being beaten back with an ash stick announced the appearance of a short, stocky woman in tweeds wearing a Burberry jacket and stout, clumpy shoes.

She smoked a pipe, and her face was determined.

The woman held a basket lined with a tea towel. She wandered off the track amongst the maidenhair ferns.

The girls, meanwhile, lost no time and, taking care not to make a din, made their way through the woodland undergrowth heading for Flo Dainty's house on the green. Miss Shelley, according to a neighbour, Mr Clairmont, one of Aunt Medley's church cronies and member of the parish council, went for her stroll in the woods regularly after lunch at half one most days. She would be up here for twenty minutes or so, and that was their window of opportunity.

Tears of gratitude were streaming down Flo Dainty's cheeks; Flo was willing herself to reach out and embrace each committed girl in turn. Alas, her arms felt too weak and feeble, her mind swimming, too dithery to offer more than an enthusiastic nodding towards the wide-open front door, for she knew, and was totally aware, she was about to be kidnapped in the nicest possible sense by a trio of friends. Saved from a greedy companion, impatient for her to die, a conniving bully, a maniac who wished to poison her system and gain possession of Flo's beloved collection of valuable antiques crowding the rooms of the Georgian house on the green, accumulated over a lifetime, some sentimental gifts from her wealthy father, bless him ...

Betty Zmunx snatched the scrawled message from her pinafore pocket and kissed Miss Dainty on the forehead. The dear lady's troubles were over. She would soon have no need of a wheeled bath chair once the poison had been reduced in her system.

The contraption was hard to steer, the single front wheel liable to pitch to the right causing the bath chair to topple over. Holding firmly onto the steering handle, Betty just about managed to keep it in a straight line, first along the passage, secondly jogged down the front step, next trundling away across the tufty grass, Flo happily waving at any neighbour inclined to be nosy.

As luck would have it, P.C. Johns, the village constable, was out on his rounds and only too delighted to stop awhile and chat with the group, unsuspecting of the bombshell about to explode on his patch.

Dismounting, he wheeled his bike across the green and bid good day. Consequently, he listened patiently while Betty stabbed her finger up at the woods, also showing him Flo's plea for help and explaining her shocking discovery at the village library.

"This is very serious." Flo nodded agreement, grasping his hand. "I shall arrest the woman, keep her detained. Betty, ask the postmistress, Dorcas Hardy, to telegraph for a police detective to come urgently from Wellingford H.Q. I will guard the house, make sure nothing is moved, nor touched. I will lock Miss Shelley up in the cellar if needs be. Attempted murder by poisoning is a capital offence. Thank goodness you girls were in time. Those books Miss Shelley loaned from the library, let me take a note of the titles, if you please, Miss Zmunx."

"Mrs Pullick's *What to Avoid when Picking Mushrooms, Poisonous Plants and Mushrooms of Great Britain, The Mushroom Gatherers' Companion – What not to pick,*" the girl replied, preparing with the others to wheel the old lady off to the nearby hotel run by Flo's friends, Alice and Bert Chard, who would supervise the doctor's visit and make sure she was safe and well-cared-for for the next fortnight until she was well enough to return home to her beloved antiques.

CHAPTER

3

Mrs Telford's Case

It had been a cold night, "Poor, dear Mrs Telford," said Aunt Medley, cleaning away the breakfast things. "Winter is always the worst time for the elderly. The woman is, according to Dr McNee, 'suffering acute depression' brought on by a flock of starlings that just invaded her garden and are determined to stay put. The eternal squabbling, the whooping whistles, leave her petrified, she just won't leave the house, afraid they will attack her. She has, in medical jargon, reached the delusional stage, even to the point of believing a robin tapped its beak on the window and spoke to her in a human voice demanding more mild cheese and biscuit crumbs."

"A nervous breakdown?"

"What else can it be? The flock of bickering birds taking over the garden has all got too much for her. She feels hemmed in, unable to cope."

"Starlings are certainly messy and high- spirited, an aggressively playful species – voracious feeders with fast metabolisms," said Mother.

"Like blue tits – fast metabolisms, I mean."

Mrs Zmunx nodded. "But *ganging up* against Mrs Telford, using their combined bird-brain wits to somehow *intimidate* her, congregating on the lawn and bird table with a sinister purpose, is like the talking robin – all rather silly."

"Dr McNee puts it down to a specific phobia – but starlings do swamp the bird table and are terrible bullies."

"No, they are merely high-spirited."

"We agree to disagree." Betty, who had been out

walking her dog, burst into the parlour. After towelling her Scotch terrier, Bertie, and wiping his paws, she ran upstairs to read the latest copy of *The Strand* magazine, to devour yet another Sherlock adventure by A.C. Doyle, this one was rather bloodthirsty and not for the squeamish, called 'The Engineer's Thumb'. The girl soon became entranced by the story.

Constable Johns, the village policeman, a family friend, called round at ten with an Inspector Haddock. They accepted a cup of milky, Camp coffee from Mother. His main purpose was to show them a wanted poster, the mugshot of an ugly, unshaven, bovine sort with piggy eyes, close-cropped hair, a wide, rubbery-lipped mouth and a podgy nose.

"One Wilfred Pockersgill," said he, "wanted in the county for robbing old ladies, using a knife, "A very unsavoury fella. Hamlets and villages are his target. The police want him behind bars. Inspector Haddock, from Wellingford C.I.D., received information from a member of the public that Pockersgill was last seen boarding a horse bus, a No.37A, at Wormley parish church stop."

"Gracious heavens," exclaimed the aunt. "The No.37A passes through our village – is he here, at large in Glim Glumswick, d'yer mean?"

"Now don't overly concern yourselves, ladies – I myself, Inspector Haddock, am a detective heading a team who are presently gathered at the police house. I must emphasise, I assure you the public are safe under my stewardship. We are only making enquiries."

"I don't like the sound of that," confided Aunt Medley in a whisper to her sister.

"Won't you have another biscuit?" said Mother brightly, offering the tin.

"Thank you, I will." The lofty inspector helped himself.

"Ah, Betty," said P.C. Johns, as the girl came rushing down the stairs, jumping the last three. "Inspector Haddock, may I introduce you to our junior 'tec," the fat policeman beamed, so proud of his long association with the 'Childhood Sleuth of Glim Glumswick'. "The clever girl I was telling you about who has assisted me in the past."

"Really," said Haddock sniffily. "P'raps we should be going, Johns. Junior 'tec indeed — a mere schoolgirl," he muttered derisively. "Good day, ladies. The sooner we catch Wilfred Pockersgill the better. I trust you, Mrs Zmunx, and your sister Miss Medley, shall remain vigilant."

"Of course, Inspector."

As they got to the garden gate of the Zmunxs' thatched brick and half-timbered cottage, P.C. Johns continued enthusing about the girl.

"That Betty has a special talent, Inspector, her powers of observation are first-rate."

"Rubbish. A youngster, a schoolgirl sleuth-hound. I beg to disagree, piffle, 'The Missing Violin', 'A Message in a Book', what nonsense you talk, P.C. Johns. Are these trifling cases really masterly examples of deductive reasoning worthy of my attention?"

"I tell you, sir, she's worth watching," the officer replied emphatically, unfazed by his superior's negativity.

They hurried off down Old Pasture Lane in the direction of the village High Street.

Winnie White and Betty decided that day, as a good turn, a good deed, to visit the poor, depressed Mrs Telford at noon. The old woman could do with company, with cheering up, they supposed. 'Brownie points were to be gained showing kindness to those less fortunate than ourselves – to be under a depression or black mood', as Dr Watson was fond of repeating when referring to his colleague's own mental dips, was not very nice for the person afflicted.

"Starlings are very noisy *and messy*, aren't they?" commented Winnie White as they approached the house. "But they have such adorable cheeky faces."

Oh dear, when the girls reached the front gate, they could see curtains were drawn and the place had a sad ambience about it, but Betty had seen a chimney pot smoking, so Mrs Telford was clearly at home, if shut indoors – herself against the world, more crucially, the dreaded starlings.

"Let's try the garden – the back door," suggested Winnie.

What a surprise, not only loads of starlings, but crows and magpies were swarming on and around the bird table, and no wonder, for a couple of tempting, fatty bones had been hung on hooks, and

was that a greasy bacon rind the birds were gorging on and squabbling over?

The bones were being stripped of their flesh by hungry, grateful beaks, for it was January and very bitter, dregs of snow on the ground. Besides the enormous amount of attracted birds, Zmunx was struck by a similarity, something last seen in the schoolhouse classroom. Seized by a hunch, she grew ever more curious and pulled from her bag a six- inch ruler, her notepad and a sharp HB pencil to make some brief sketches. Moving swiftly through the carpet of squabbling birds to attain a closer glimpse of the bird table, the meaty bones in particular, one specimen of which she took great care in measuring.

"Our teacher, Miss Terns', anatomical skeleton," she murmured. "Something rings similar, Winnie."

"What?" answered her friend vaguely, sucking on a pineapple sweet, noticing the net curtains shift slightly in one of the lower windows of Mrs Telford's cottage.

Glim Glumswick Echo – JAN 15th, 1901

A local resident, a Mrs Telford, has been taken into care after police broke into her house and found the dismembered remains of a wanted criminal down in the cellar. The woman diagnosed suffering acute depression, in a delusional state, had apparently mistaken an intruder for a giant starling and violently attacked him with a knife. The police are full of praise, commending the prompt action of a young, unnamed girl who brought the matter to the attention of Inspector Haddock of Wellingford C.I.D. Mrs Telford had begun feeding body parts of the said Pockersgill to the birds. Further details are deemed of a far too distressing and gruesome a nature to impart to our readers.

CHAPTER

4

School Bag

The last lesson of the day at the height of summer, a boiling hot August, everyone wilting in the heat, was uphill work for any teacher, but Miss Tern, with her long, luxuriant hair gathered and pinned at the back, looking very cool and pretty in her grey-and-white striped dress and blouse with mutton-chop sleeves, had latched onto a subject of interest, and so far the pupils in her charge remained attentive.

"Mummy's an awful queer name, isn't it?" offered John Byford from the back of the class, eyes downturned, in open-cloth shirt, shabby green corduroys, doing a nervy shuffle on the parquet floor with his hobnail boots. "If he were a bloke, this Pharaoh King wotsit, it don't sound right. Sounds allus wrong t'me."

"To mummify in ancient Egypt meant to preserve a body by embalming and wrapping it up. The word *mummy* comes from the original Arabic for 'embalmed body'," said the form teacher primly, wanting to move things on, "Now, tell me class, what animals can you see on page eight of the Egyptian picture book?"

"Elephants."

"Camels."

"Cows wi' horns."

"Well done, form. How many Nile Geese are there? Count back from the group of palm trees."

"Crikey, what about the mummy's curse?" Came another interruption.

The recently publicised Tutankhamen tomb excavation sprung to mind. The teacher was impressed how ideas were percolating in her class.

"Good point, Mullins," she agreed, "does the mummy somehow return, is it's malign influence felt?"

Julie Pottle swept back her hair from her flushed, hot face, staring resolutely at the blackboard. It was because of this 'curse rage', the public interest, that the British Museum had begun selling printed tin mummy pencil cases that clipped in two halves. Julie's parents had bought her one which she kept in her school bag.

The bell clanged – school finished for the day.

Miss Tern, joined by Mrs Plumb, cautioned calm as everyone made a dash for the playground.

Over by the school gates Julie Pottle was sobbing, crying her eyes out – kids hurrying past. Betty hurried over.

"It's my canary, she's gone and died," the girl whimpered, her round, apple- blossom cheeks smudged with streaky tears. "School helped me forget, but what shall I ever do without my Elsphet?"

The girl had stopped blubbering, more at the snuffles stage.

"Nothing a strawberry ice won't cure," said Betty positively. School was over, play ruled so far as she was concerned. "C'mon Julie, run you to the sweet shop."

***

Aunt Medley and Edwina Zmunx were just clearing away the tea things, Mrs Appleton, their domestic, about to depart for home, snapping her handbag shut, straightening her hat, when Winnie White came bounding into the parlour at Old Pasture Cottage. She had been running fast with her little fox terrier which was panting; she herself gave urgent gasps as she spoke. Aunt Medley set a bowl of water down for the dog, which lapped it up gratefully. Although it was evening, the heat had not abated, the sun shone stronger than ever. Most folk were collapsed on sofas or deckchairs, praying for a thunderstorm, a drop of rain.

"Betty's got to come quickly," she implored. "Julie Pottle's just wandered off. Her mum's worried."

"Betty!" Mother called upstairs to the loft, fully sensing the emergency. Her daughter came clumping down the staircase, wearing a pinafore over her flowery print dress.

"Heard you, Winnie. Wonder where Julie's got to?" She fixed her straw bonnet to the back of her head, as was the fashion, tying it beneath her chin, then searched for the dog lead.

"Mrs Pottle wonders where all her jewellery's gone. It was on her dressing table," said Winnie, "so it's serious."

"Ma, I'm taking Bertie for a walk."

"Very well, dear. Don't stay out too long. Your homework needs attention. I do hope Mrs Pottle's not too distressed. You could do with checking at Lizzie's place, or Polly Housman's in Leaf Lane."

"Will do."

The Pottles lived in a half-timbered, red brick, Queen Ann-style house at the top end of Glim Glumswick High Street. It had a clay-tiled roof, pointed gables and dormer windows. This pleasing residence was situated close to the kerb, separated from the road only by a very narrow strip of pavement.

The girls were seen from the window, the front door opened; Mrs Pottle anxious for news. "You know my Julie; this just isn't like her, Betty, to go off without telling me."

"She was upset after school about Elsphet, of course. How did she seem at tea?" asked Winnie, kneeling to pat the dog.

"Seemed a bit blotto," shrugged Mrs Pottle, showing the girls into the low-beamed sitting room. "The hot weather, I s'pect. Gracious, all of us are suffering under this heatwave. Of course, the death of her pet canary must have something to do with it; you know how my daughter doted on that pretty yellow bird, but where can my jewellery have got to?"

Everyone instinctively turned their gaze to consider the now empty, forlorn cage in the sitting room, the water bowl, dowelling perch, swing and oval dangling mirror still in place, the gritty layer of paper on the bottom.

"She's obviously stolen my jewellery, which is most worrying. She's never behaved like this before."

Betty was seized by an idea. "Mrs Pottle, might I take a peep inside Julie's school bag, the blue one with the white cord?"

"What? Oh, it's out here in the passage, dear, hooked on the hall stand. My rings and brooches are gone, of course. Wilbert, my husband, shall be livid when he returns from work, but my darling little girl, what could have become of her? At this rate I shall have to inform P.C. Johns at the police house."

"Hmmm," proposed Betty. "Just let me look in her school bag a mo', will you Mrs Pottle?"

Making the dogs bark and yap joyously, to chase their tails, Betty Zmunx snatched the bag and energetically turned it upside down, spilling the entire contents on the table. Out fell a chewed apple core, orange peel, sweet wrappers, sorrel leaves, a lined school exercise book, followed by a vigorous shake and the clatter of HB and colour pencils, one rubber, pencil sharpener, shavings, six-inch ruler, but *definitely no colourful printed tin mummy pencil case* that prised in half, moulded in the shape of a pharaoh.

Betty and Winnie White walked their dogs, emerging from a country lane steeply banked into the field margins, forced to step quickly onto the verge to wait for a pony chaise driven by a local farmer's wife to pass, clopping up the dust; it was still quite hot, and the sun was blazing. The girls quickly crossed Robin Post Lane, the schoolhouse now in prospect. If Betty's hunch proved correct, Julie Pottle would soon be home with her mother.

The girls leaned over the wall. Julie appeared to be at play in the schoolyard's sandpit, but on closer scrutiny, the culture of ancient Egypt had come alive in Glim Glumswick, infiltrated into English village life, for she was huddled before a scooped-out, make-believe tomb, her mother's jewels carefully arranged inside, a half brick waiting to seal the tomb entrance.

A sarcophagus, the printed tin mummy pencil case in the image of a pharaoh, housed the body. It lay half open, a glimpse of an upturned bird's beak and yellow feathers visible within. The canary in repose, Elsphet risen in rank to a sacred, noble princess bathed in nytron.

Out and about, her collecting tin rattling with pennies and halfpennies all in aid of the church restoration fund, Betty was fortunate to bump into her near neighbour, the eccentric local historian, Professor Lallington. Wearing a panama hat and white tropical suit, he was venturing into the public library. He was intrigued to hear about the canary.

"Most singular," said he, puffing on his gargoyle pipe. "I have it on good authority that in Egypt a bird can be regarded in the desert, as the Arabs say, *Bakh Heit*, a luck bringer, a good omen. Let us take the case of Carter in charge of this Tutankhamen dig, who, at the start of the season, brought along a little songbird to accompany him. 'He is lucky,' said the work gang, 'he sings so sweetly.' The bird was kept in a cage inside his tent.

"Alas, at the very time the door to the inner chamber was about to be opened, it was reported a cobra, the symbol of royalty and protection, had got in and eaten the bird. Bang goes good luck, replaced by superstition and ill-omen for the future, a curse is responsible, the whole team affected, but not quite. You see, Betty, a telegram was sent to a spiffing ally, Lady Evelyn Herbert, a no-nonsense, tweedy type who drove over the desert from Cairo in her Austin motor saloon bearing a canary to replace the cobra's luncheon snack. Cheerfulness and equilibrium restored, the curse was forgotten. The king's soon-to-be discovered burial chamber, full of gold and splendour, was henceforth nicknamed *Bab-el-Asfour* – 'The Tomb of the Bird'."

CHAPTER

5

Winter Visitors

Winter settled early on the village that year. Freezing temperatures took hold just before Christmas and did not abate until early March. The first significant snowfall fell on the day before Christmas Eve.

More and more snow followed and lasted for ages, causing disruption for adults, and fun and thrills for children for, as the schoolhouse was closed, they were able to toboggan and skate, and throw snowballs at each other to their hearts content.

They also built snowmen – the favoured style being a traditional, roughly-patted, 'double snow boulder' head and body type with a carrot nose and twigs for limbs. For the finishing touches the children would use dad's old pipe and hat, a stripy scarf, and coal chips for eyes and buttons.

As the big freeze continued, with yet another bitterly cold day in prospect, rosy-cheeked Betty, well wrapped up against the chill wearing her beaver-skin hat and three-quarter length coat, was trudging along by the drystone walling. For some reason unknown, she felt a strong pull to visit the

churchyard.

Since her weekend spent at Larna Amberley's house, Mulberry Manor, Betty had become accustomed to working with Tudor Sefton – the young ghost-girl who frustrated and annoyed Larna's grandmother with her constant wanderings in search of a lost snuff box.

Tudor's unique form of transport – a flying coffin. A bond instantly existed, a natural and effortless kinship beyond the limited view of what a ghost should be like.

Walking beneath the lychgate, making her way up towards Glim Glumswick church, Betty saw, under an overcast sky, Mr Ralphs – the sexton – busy shovelling snow, scraping the path outside the porch to be later spread with cinders, an old slop bucket filled with collected fireplace ash nearby. She continued round, stepping across, drawn to a particular grave.

After dusting fluffy snow from the stone slab marking the burial place with her glove, Betty intuitively stood very still at the foot of the grave putting every ounce of attention into focusing on the epitaph carved on the face of the granite headstone. The words written in memory of a person who had died long ago.

After only a short interval, something very odd happened – the letters jumbled up and began rearranging themselves forming a definite readable directive:

Dearest Betty

Mrs Creech wants to 'message' you on her tablet. Her plot is further along the path on the right-hand side near a litter bin, you can't miss it.

P.S. I'm one of Tudor Sefton's old

mates, Anne of Barstow.

Unperturbed by this strange event, Betty pulled her scarf snugly over her nose and set off – her stout, nail-studded boots sinking into the snowy crust along the verge. Once she had located Mrs Creech's headstone, keeping her mind focused, she keenly awaited a message.

Letters soon started dancing about, swirling into one another, the sepulchral text on the granite face becoming transformed.

This is awfullish dull of me, dear,

and I know you will think me a bit

dotty, but could you explain this,

please – how can a snowman move all by

itself? Take the one over on the

vicarage lawn, for example – it went

out early this morning

and shut the gate behind it!
Regards

Mrs Eunice Creech (deceased)

Not long after, the wording on the headstone

returned to normal, replaced by a respectful ode originally chiselled by the stone mason of the day. This left Betty genuinely puzzled, wondering if this was a joke at her expense, the result of some spirit, perhaps.

But evidence was quickly forthcoming, backing up Mrs Creech's message, for the fat policeman, the amiable village constable, P.C. Johns, was at that

moment crossing the road on his way to the vicarage to discuss that same matter.

"Betty, I've had umpteen reports of snowmen. Snowmen that should, by rights, be solidly stood in gardens and the school playground, but have come alive and been witnessed as such. Take this statement by Mrs Bunn, for instance!" Unbuttoning his tunic pocket, the constable snatched out his notepad scowling at the jottings. "'I was walking along Upper Park Road, on my way to the shops, when I saw a pair of snowmen coming towards me — you know, carrot nosed, wearing tatty hats and scarves with twig limbs. One, who was smoking a pipe, lifted up his twig arm and politely doffed his battered trilby to me.

"'Good morning, madam,' says "he", or "it", pleasantly. 'A most agreeable day to be outdoors. I see so many plumes of smoke coming out of cottage chimney pots. How on earth anyone of you villagers can abide the heat of coal fires on a day like this escapes me.'

"Mrs Bunn went onto compliment one gentleman snowman on his red-spotted woollen scarf before hurrying off in search of the police house, for she knew not what to make of the encounter."

"I am reliably informed the snowman on the vicarage lawn has gone missing," said the girl.

"That makes nine altogether: Vic and Ethel Chailey at number forty-two; little Alfred and Mavis Simms at Lamb Cottage; Lucy Smollet at number three. Oh, the list children have given me of missing snowman ... This peculiar migration from back gardens to appearing on the High Street and round about Glim Glumswick... They all appear to be very civil. There's been no reports of threatening behaviour towards the public – so far, anyway. The snowmen, it seems, are going out of their way to be polite and sociable to anyone they meet."

"But wait a mo," pointed out Betty, "they can't walk, can they? How do they jolly well get about, open garden gates?"

"All who see them say they skim above the ground effortlessly and silently. They can coordinate movements of their twig limbs, doff their hats in greeting, smoke pipes and speak the Queen's English."

"Stuff that! There must be some explanation – boys operating them," Betty retorted, somewhat brusquely.

"Just consider this, Betty. Hilda Atwell and a Miss Smith of Leaf Lane spoke to me earlier of their first encounter which I duly noted down. 'Ladies, forgive my forwardness,' a snowman remarked, gliding along the pavement. 'But it seems to us you village folk are far too wrapped up. Take off your clothes, abandon yourselves to the cold.'

"Another snowman is quoted as saying, while ingratiating himself to an elderly spinster he had helped cross the icy road. *She*, perhaps susceptible to flattery, clung onto his birch twig arm drinking in every word. *He*, afterwards doffing his shapeless round hat in a mark of good fellowship. '*Nakedly* embrace the ice and snow like we do, my dear. Enjoy this lovely weather while it lasts. Why bother with the expense of coal or paraffin – let the house *freeze*, be liberated from the constraints of heat.'"

After recounting these instances to Betty, P.C. Johns hurried off to visit the Rev Smithson at the rectory. Meanwhile, the junior sleuth set off to the High Street, determined to see one of these snowmen for herself. She suspected this mild hysteria was being created by, basically, a wire cage or framework, similar to the outmoded ladies fashion of steel crinolines – or hoops worn to bolster petticoats and skirts – smothered in plaster of Paris, or papier mâché, thickly spread over gauze and painted. The finished constructions enabling a boy to steer what was, after all, a glorified go-cart.

She was in luck. No sooner in sight of the public library beyond the shops, a snowman, this one bowler-hatted, came skimming up beside her. Raising a twig hand, he proffered advice.

"Don't be in such an awful hurry, miss. There's a

patch of ice froze up yonder making the pavement treacherous to the untrained eye. Do watch your step."

"I am perfectly capable of working that out for myself, thank you," said Betty, shrewdly taking full advantage of the close proximity to test her theory. She brushed her glove against the side of the snowman.

Her fingers felt frozen – real powdery snow fell away, but the good Samaritan was not done with her yet.

"If it doesn't snow again tonight, do watch out for black ice." The girl found this goody-goody attitude mildly patronising, but the fact the snowman was talking and able to move about by its own propulsion baffled her.

Over the coming days, more good deeds came to be reported in the papers, the *Glim Glumswick Echo*, on the whole, positive:

SNOWMAN SAVES MAN'S LIFE

A victim of a road traffic accident was stretchered to the cottage hospital – not having to await a horse-ambulance, but being 'skimmed' fast and efficiently, above ground level, by two snowmen. "A most comfortable way to travel," attested a Mr Livesey, who was treated for a fractured ankle and had his head bandaged.

SNOWMAN SAVES THE DAY – RAILWAY
TRAGEDY AVERTED

A runaway train was brought to a standstill thanks to the quick reactions of a number of snowmen who were able to jump into the firebox and down the locomotive's chimney, damping down flames, dousing the furnace fire causing all mechanical propulsion to cease.

Numerous elderly folk were guided and kept safe from dangerous icy pavements by amiable snowman 'lookouts' on hand to help and advise, encouraging the oldens to get out and about and enjoy the below-freezing temperatures while they lasted — not stay closeted indoors. Local children were now able to hop onto the backs of snowmen for exciting rides.

On the whole, it must be said, humans and

snowmen in Glim Glumswick seemed, in a very short time, to be achieving a perfect harmony, a compatible equilibrium suiting both parties, but then …

'Old Stumpy', the gypsy, and a local birdwatcher, Mr Porter, were the first to record the mass deaths of wild birds and animals found frozen in the woods along by Prudie Lane. Stuck fast to branches of trees and the woodland floor – shrews, stoats, squirrels and foxes exhibiting rictus – fangy grins – unusually, eyes not black but pale blue, a remarkable ocular change brought about by the calamitous effects of a core of intense cold emanating from some central vicinity of the woods transforming the climate with temperatures as low as -60° centigrade, to mirror those of a polar ice cap, causing trees to become brittle and snap. The gypsies unable to withstand the trough of low pressure abandoned camp and headed for another village, taking their caravans with them.

By this time, snowmen missing from gardens increased from nine to fifteen. Children's happy handiwork, a source of such joy and competition amongst the youngsters of the village, were on the move – not invading the village, exactly ... more carefully observing.

'These abnormally low temperatures attributed to the woods are set to engulf as all,'

Warned Professor Lallington in a newsletter distributed secretly to householders.

'The cold spot is diffusing and slowly creeping our way. I advise residents to remain vigilant, what in reality is their purpose for being here? We must question the snowmen's motive for gaining the trust and sympathy of the local populace. This nucleus of intolerable icy-cold emanating from the woods must

be investigated further. Who, or what, exactly are these beings adopting the snowmen as an outer guise?'

A plan was hatched, and it was decided the village constable, P.C. Johns, Professor Lallington and Betty – and her best chum, Winnie White – should, at the earliest opportunity, try to infiltrate the central woods. See what, if anything, was to be discovered. By wearing layers of thick winter coats, hot water bottles strapped close to their skin, it was hoped a brief reconnaissance would be possible. Betty and Winnie were to take sketch pads, P.C. Johns a truncheon in case of arrests, and Professor Lallington his curved tobacco pipe for added warmth.

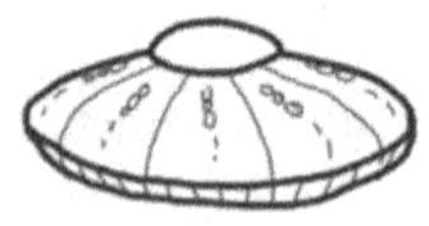

Betty Zmunx's sketch of the saucer-like object

found in the woods that vanished overnight.

Most people in the village were relieved when a general thaw set in. Temperatures began to rise, and the winter's snow melted. Nothing more was seen of the beneficent snowmen that year.

TWELVE YEARS OLD

CHAPTER

Trip To Hamleys

Upon a chilly day in December, under a drab sky, the Zmunx's gathered to catch the train to Paddington, spending a day out in town where could be visited stores such as Peter Robinson's, D.H. Evans, Liberty's and Harrods, and Maple's Furniture Emporium where this year Mother ordered a rosewood bureau to be delivered home.

Betty's undoubted favourite was Hamleys at No. 188–196 Regent Street, purportedly the world's largest toy store, dwarfing all other toy stores in the empire.

Christmas approaching, fog inevitably blanketed the capital. Peasoupers, as they were called, made travel by public omnibus through teeming traffic, even by motor buses with their hard tyres, slow and tedious. Alternatively, ideal for West End theatres and shops, the Central London Circle line offered travel by the so-called multiple units, electrified trains which travelled swiftly and efficiently from Liverpool Street through to Tottenham Court Road and Oxford Circus, but fog or no fog, window shopping, visiting the palatial department stores with electrically lit shopfronts was wildly exciting to Betty.

The underground train, however, proved crowded and stuffy. Mother and Aunt Medley were offered seats right away by exceptionally gallant young city clerks, but Betty Zmunx declined her mother's knee, choosing to stand crushed in with other passengers rocking to and fro with the carriage as it rattled through subterranean tunnels.

Awkwardly placed, the girl, nonetheless, due to her height was drawn to overhear a whispered conversation between two German gentlemen sat

close by, concealed behind upraised broadsheets, one of the newspapers peculiarly upside down. Betty's face was hot, she felt crushed-in, yet despite her discomfort was intrigued by what she perceived to be conspiratorial.

The *Daily Telegraph* spoke forth: "Ach, Karl, tonight, tonight we shall crack such a crib, as the Englander cockney scoundrel is fond of saying. All is perfectly in place, ja!"

"How can we fail, my dear Franz?" the upside-down newspaper replied jubilantly. "The accounts office, on the ground floor."

At Oxford Circus everyone got off and Betty was able to catch a glimpse of the pair of foreign gentlemen, finely dressed in their tweed Bavarian hunting jackets and alpine smartly- brimmed hats with a feather slid in the band.

By mid-afternoon, tramping about Liberty's, D.H. Evans and Peter Robinson's, a splendid lunch of steak

and kidney pudding, apple pie and cream to follow,
for a shilling each at a cook-shop along Oxford Street,
the Zmunx's buoyed up by purchases of gifts, already
weighed under by parcels and bulging shopping
bags, crossed to the east side of foggy Regents
Street, chock-a- block with a mix of slow moving,
lamp-lit motors, hansom cabs, delivery box carts and
private carriages, joining a throng of children, adults

in tow, about to enter the portals of Hamleys store.

An Aladdin's cave. Three full floors displaying every make of doll, dolls' prams, dolls' houses, teddy bears, model train sets, automobiles, lead farm animals, cut-out theatres, boxed Bengal lancers, forts, cannon that fired pellets, boxed games, Ludo, steam and sail craft, jigsaws, tops, hoops, roller skates and much, much more, painted tin toys set in motion by clockwork particularly favourite with boys. This year, floor displays of gadgets, automata were, frankly, awesome.

Prompted by Mother to check the dolls' house accessories, a selection of beautifully made Welsh dressers, displaying minute little hand-painted knick-knacks, the detail exquisite, caught her eye. But gracious, the cost! Nine shillings! Six for the dresser, three for the knick-knacks. Nine whole shillings — much too much. Ma had already forked out for pair of kid gloves and a fur-collared coat. A bustle of people were now forming, for the three o'clock automata display, over the way.

"The German and Swiss are the world leaders in automata," barked a gentleman. "Nobody can touch them. We are fortunate at Hamleys to have Karl Werther and Franz Kemph, engineering attendants who will work on all night if they have to, to ensure these mechanical marvels run properly over the Christmas period. Ah, hush, Miss Timkins, the red locomotive and nativity scene nearby are about to start up."

By now, Betty Zmunx, her mother, Edwina, and Aunt Medley had joined a crowd gathering expectantly. Bang on three, the automata whirred into action. A gleaming, bright-red locomotive festooned with brass, the cab big enough for a grown boy to sit in, towing a single truck, was first to mechanically function, a headlamp switched on, a whistle tooted, everyone gasped in wonder. Puffs of smoke clouds realistically issued from its green chimney accompanied by a distinctive chuff-chuff-chuffing. Shiny brass wheels bolted to piston rods began to turn. Most remarkable of all, the head of the engine driver wearing a jaunty leather cap, the mannequin so lifelike in work overalls it was hard to determine whether it was real or not, began to rotate in a way to gaze at the spectators, winking and grinning at everybody, much slicker and less spooky than a ventriloquist's dummy. A friendly hand waved from the cab and the crowd of children waved back, totally believing in the automaton.

Nearby, the life-size nativity scene set in a manger likewise became automated, the three turbaned kings of the Orient nodding and offering gifts, cows and sheep doing likewise, their heads emitting moo and baa sounds most convincingly.

The automata were brilliant and yet Betty could not help recalling the hushed conversation she overheard in the underground train, the conspiratorial newspapers, one plainly upside down. She gripped her duck-handled brolly firmly and headed over to where the floor manager and a female assistant stood talking.

"Excuse me, might I have a word?" said the girl, tugging at the gentleman's frock coat.

"Are you lost? Chin up, my name is Braggins, I'm the floor manager. This is Miss Timkins, my assistant." The woman smiled sweetly.

"It's really, really important, Mr Braggins."

"Important, eh? Fire away." The fellow leaned down and, taking the girl very seriously, for children were treated as little adults, listened carefully while she talked into his ear, barely heard above the din of the red engine whistling and puffing away, entering its final phase. Betty did her best to make a scrupulous account of all she had overheard on the circle line train, pointing out the gentlemen behind the newspapers were undoubtedly Germans referred to as Karl and Franz.

"I say, gracious me, that does sound rather queer," said he. "Very well, step this way, miss; you say that's your mother and auntie presently stood behind the elderly country parson in gaiters leaning on his umbrella. Miss Timkins, be good enough to fetch them, could you, then we'll pop upstairs sharpish to see the chairman."

Chairman's office: 3.28

Enshrined in his oak-panelled sanctum, Mr Hamley, on being suitably briefed, beckoned the Zmunx's be seated. Wearing a fine, tailored frock coat, pinstriped trousers and trendy mauve spats, the kindly old gentleman took his place behind his imposing desk and allowed coffee to be served with long- practised finesse by his male secretary; a plate of Huntley & Palmers biscuits was passed round.

"Ladies, delighted I'm sure," said he, placing his podgy hands comfortably on his immense paunch. "My wife, bless her, pointed out to me last weekend an article in *Country Life* magazine which aye enjoyed immensely," he drawled. "So you are the Betty Zmunx featured, Glim Glumswick's junior sleuth, commended so highly by the county's superintendent, Colonel Clinkworthy. Your career so far is quate extraordinary, 'The Canary Case', 'The Old Violin Wotnot' gone into some detail. Quate remarkable for a youngster. Although I take exception to Colonel Clinkworthy's comments on women being one day allowed to join the police force, to train in the detective branch, that's going too far," the chairman nibbled on his biscuit before continuing. "Now, Miss Zmunx, what's this you say about Mr Werther and Mr Kemph? Seem alright fellas t'me. Heads screwed on, always polite to my staff, quate helpful, wot!"

"Sir," Betty implored. "Is it correct that your weekly takings are kept in a company safe, transferred to the Town & Counties bank in the morning, as Mr Braggins suggests?"

"Aahhh'm, absolutely – guards, y'know." He tapped the ridge of his nose confidentially.

"The bank sends a special box van, y'see. Our accounts department is on the ground floor. All done very discreetly an' proper. Never had no criminal bother so far, wot!"

"My dear Chairman," implored Braggins, beside himself with concern. "That could be all about to change – a plot to rob Hamleys. If what Miss Zmunx told me is correct, and I'm sure it is, we have an insider job. The German automata mechanics intend to steal the weekly takings; the accounts department is to be burgled."

"B-b-b-b-burgled?" stuttered the shocked chairman, spitting biscuit crumbs all over the desk. "The week's takings, thousands of pounds, but how? Hamleys? Never, never in my life, I say."

No time was to be lost. Mr Hamley sprang into action; although big and bulky, he was extremely light-footed. Yes, it must be admitted the chairman was bombastic, ruthless, pompous even, but rightly so. Why, he owned the entire store, and every department that went with it. Stupid he was not, so he stood by Betty's word.

"I think I have an idea how they intend to rob the safe," said Betty, glancing at her mother. Without further ado everyone flew out of the chairman's office and hurried downstairs into the crowd of shoppers.

Gripping the duck handle of her folded brolly in a determined way, the clever girl barged through people to reach the gleaming red engine on display. Frowning, she was at odds with the smiling children in search of toys. On tiptoe, ignoring the dummy of the engine driver, she leaned over the simplistic cab. Above the fake firebox doors, a puzzling array of push/pull stops like on a church organ, at first appearance merely intended for show. Might they in fact work? This gave Betty an idea: the green stop, presumably green for 'GO'. She prepared to tug it out.

"Silly, I know, but these knobs and buttons must have something to do with it."

"To do with what, Miss Zmunx?" asked the chairman, totally mystified, flocking round with the others anxious to make inroads, Miss Timkins taking down notes.

"Controlling those automata."

"Which automata?" queried Mother, at a loss. "Do speak more concisely, dear, not in riddles," said Aunt Medley sternly, but all was shortly revealed when Betty boldly tugged out the green stopper. Then, an amazing thing occurred.

The Three Wise Men bearing gifts of gold, frankincense, and myrrh, stood static over by the crib at the nativity scene, jerkily started to function, discarding their ornate caskets. The first robed and turbaned king, so realistically built it might have been human, outstretched its mechanical arm. The right hand, constructed of a hardened wax substance, flipped open at the wrist. It was hinged, clockwork cogs in operation. A drill and bit extended telescopically, starting to activate, whir round and round.

Another of the turbaned Oriental kings likewise abandoned its gift casket. Stretching out its arm, beneath the flesh tone of the waxy finish was a clever system of wires, clockwork pulleys and steel rods engaged as the hand unclipped at the wrist, flapping open. Extraordinary to relate, a gas blowtorch extended, flaming into life.

The third Wise Man, possessing similar metallic components, revealed a lethal cutting implement. When shoppers noticed the drill and the flare of the blowtorch, a mild panic ensued. The Three Wise Men proceeded to jerkily advance directly across the shop floor, heading for the accounts department over the way; they had been somehow pre-programmed to do this.

Meanwhile, the girl focused her whole attention on the single truck, the tender, lifting out, with the help of Aunt Medley, an entire square of lumpy fake coal that clipped away easily, only to find a big battery beneath. Curious, without thinking, filled with childish glee, not knowing exactly why and totally uncaring of the risk, she began to stab repeatedly at one of the electrodes on top of the battery with the tip of her duck-handled brolly. The metal ferule, on contact, caused an explosion of sparks, a blue lightning flame, an acrid pong filling the shop floor.

Luckily, thanks to Mother dragging her back in the nick of time, Betty was prevented from being electrocuted. Her beloved duck-handled brolly, alas, burned to a crisp, beyond repair. But there were compensations. Everyone watched with relief as the two figures of the nativity scene, heading jerkily towards the office door, the kings from the Orient, collapsed in a useless heap, smoke escaping, billowing from their nostrils and from beneath their handsome bejewelled turbans, the drill bit, winding to a standstill, the flaring gas jet extinguished, shut off, no longer lethal on human contact.

The chairman, Mr Hamley, looked delighted. "Hamleys ten – burglars nil, wot-wot. Thanks to Miss Zmunx, Glim Glumswick's childhood sleuth, we've won hands down. Any toy in the store is yours for the asking, my dear …" he quickly corrected himself, for

thrift was one of his main attributes, "up to ten shillings in value."

Betty showed no hesitation. "I should so like that little Welsh dresser; it's ever so expensive, Ma, nine shillings. Golly."

"Yours," insisted the chairman. "Yours, my child. Now all of us must later hop into my Rolls Royce and take tea at Claridges. Ah, Mr Braggins, you have word. So efficient my staff, wot-wot."

"Mr Chairman, sir, I can report both of the foreign gentlemen, part of a group of Germans hoodwinking us who should take part in the robbery planned for tonight, employing those, those machines to aid their nefarious purpose, breaking into the great Chubb safe at Hamleys' accounts department, stashing the weekly takings, have been restrained with the other German staff members and the whole gang placed under lock and key in our store room in the basement. Your secretary, Mr Allison, took the liberty of telegraphing Scotland Yard. A contingent of constables and a detective are on their way, I am led to understand, sir."

What news! Betty, however, together with Mother and Aunt Medley, were led by staff at a sedate pace across the floor to the dolls' house counter, where she chose the little Welsh dresser and hand-painted, minutely detailed knick-knacks. A member of Hamleys' staff boxed and wrapped the items in velvety gold paper, a red Christmas ribbon attached. Mother instantly took charge of the gift box, placing it in her shopping bag, not to be opened until Christmas morning – before church, of course.

CHAPTER

7

Plantwatch

For the last year, Mr Bunberry and Mr Gilbert have been assembling an enterprising machine from scrap and engine spare parts over at the locomotive shed workshop – using GN&SR company time and equipment. To be specific, creating a metal torso, arms, and a pair of legs. Over the way, Mr Poopson, the popular Glim Glumswick signalman, had been assisting the process – working in his own garden shed – taking care, the saucepan head swivelled round properly on greased ball-bearings. He had also, from plans, constructed, to exacting standards, the chimney helmet, breast-plate and clip-on fire basket, leaving his colleagues to fit the steam boiler and piston components.

In short, out of old iron, nuts and bolts, rivets and cannibalised mechanical parts, even coiled bedsprings adopted for suspension purposes – a 'man' had been born. The team of GN&SR railwaymen were to be congratulated.

Betty and Lucian Finn, because of their friendship with Mr Poopson, learnt early on of the venture. The children would often assist the signalman, handing him some tool if required, adjusting the vice, or tidying the workbench. Lucian was even allowed to hammer out a dent on the metal breast-plate. Mr Poopsons' garden shed that summer had been a hive of activity.

One afternoon, the machine nearing completion, Winnie White and Larna Amberly, whilst kneeling on the lawn, helped put finishing touches applying Brasso and other cleaning products, polishing the breast-plate and iron- shod boots until they gleamed under the hot sun.

Mr Nincombe Poopson and the engineers' efforts were rewarded as one day, over at the loco shed, the steam-driven man was hauled to his feet using a winch. But Alf Bunbury, wearing his dun-coloured work coat put forward a valid point.

"What bloomin' use is 'e even if 'e works – a steam boiler on legs."

"Righ', Hauling a cart of turnips, maybe summink in the agricultural line," decided Mr Gilbert.

Betty, bright as a button, was struck by an idea. She knew P.C. Johns, the village constable, had for some time been moaning of the increased crime rate. How he could do with some active support, Inspector Haddock of Wellingford CID, was having none of it and told his officer to 'get on with it – you're on a rural beat'.

Mr Poopson, Alf and Trevor liked the connection, and saw promise in the young lady's suggestion.

"Betty," said the signalman, "cycle over ta the police 'ouse orn yer bike an' fetch John's over 'ere sharpish."

Sunning himself on a deckchair when the children turned up P C Johns was not really that bothered. To be honest, he thought they were joking, but after Betty's insistence, trusting her not to pull a fast one, he put on his uniform tunic and helmet joining them peddling like billyo back to the railway sidings at Glim Glumswick station.

Messrs Poopson, Bunbury and Gilbert were waiting around and greeted him with a practical demonstration there in the loco shed. The steam man got fired up, Welsh coal, plenty of water. It took about half an hour to get full pressure.

"Very basic, see," said Mr Bunbury scowling. "We've got a leaver slides into three notches. Two twistable valve knobs, pressure gauge – speed dial – nothing could be simpler. Just point him in the right direction."

Johns saw at once the potential. His prayers had been answered. "How long will he keep going?"

"Good hour, I reckon. No trials as yet, o' course."

"Got any blue gloss?"

"Reckon there's a can under the workbench."

"And a paintbrush, ta." The officer seized the paint pot, dabbing the word 'POLICE' across the breast-plate in big capitals. Admiring of the steam contraption, the wavering flame glowing behind the orbital slits. Why, the steam man looked

intimidating – perfect for the job, an added police presence along the High Street. "You're in, mate. By jingo, you heap of junk you."

A sharp, ear-splitting whistle, like from an oversized kettle, stopped him in mid-sentence. He spoke more generously next time, while Mr Bunbury busied himself with a spanner sealing down the errant valve.

"The steam policeman is bound to impress members of the public. I'll make up a duty roster, he'll start on Monday patrolling along the High Street."

"We don't know whether he works properly yet," cautioned Mr Gilbert.

"No time like the present. Lucian, laddie, do the honours," the village constable, indicated to the single lever on the back of the machine man. The boy grinning hugely, rushed forward, tugging it into the first setting. His eyes stinging from the effusion of smoke puffing out of the chimney helmet, Lucian Finn coughed and got out of the way fast.

Clunkety-clunk, the saucepan head swivelled from side to side, the iron-shod boots engaged, it began to walk.

The next Monday, everything that could go wrong did go wrong. The patrol was a fiasco. Stumping along the High Street, accompanied by a very worried P.C. Johns on his bicycle, police steam man's clumsy control meant the extreme weight of his heavy iron-shod boots cracked pavements on impact, chipped curb stones, that showers of sparks from his fire basket set shop awnings alight and people's hats. Bumping into a lamppost outside the pharmacy, he bent it over. The noise was horrendous. Coal smuts proved disagreeable to shoppers. His route was basic, up one side of the village High Street, down the other, but then, of all the embarrassment he broke down crossing the road holding up all the traffic and frightening horses. Mechanical failure – the last straw! Due to public hostility, the trial was aborted, a cart called for.

'Useless,' the general view. 'Too noisy by far. Much too smoky'. The machine invention was winched onto the wagonette and taken back to the police house amid much scoffing, laughter from a crowd of pedestrians.

Betty felt sorry, she said as much to her mother and Aunt Medley back at the family cottage in Old Pasture Lane.

"P.S.M. was only trying, after all. His first day's patrol, now everyone's ganging up," said Betty.

"Don't be silly," replied the aunt, doing her crossword, "It's a machine, not a person. Really, you must be more grown up about these things, Betty."

P.C. Johns put him into storage, and that should have been the ignominious ending.

That afternoon the girls decided to lay down on

the grass and soak up the sun. From this vantage on the crest of the hillock, a bronze age local burial mound, Betty noticed something *different* about the valley landscape, a change. She felt sure a ring of white foliage, a vegetation surrounding the village had encroached closer to the outlying properties.

A dare to run down the hill at full pelt, however, with dogs barking, eager to compete, pushed the matter of this changed landscape more to the back of her mind.

Coming down the footpath, clambering over a style – nearly onto the main road – a young lad, Jamie Oates, whom Betty knew from the schoolhouse, was staggering about in a state of distress, clutching at his face in agony. The gang of girls was shocked to see his exposed arms and legs covered in welts, enormous blisters the size of golf balls. His swollen face, what one could see of it, erupted in a red angry rash.

"I'm afire, afire," he screamed, "boiling up I is –
'elp me, 'elp me."

'Goodness,' the girl thought, shouting for Winnie
and Lizzie to keep their distance.

Still clutching his inflamed face, sadly Jamie,
unable to stand the pain, collapsed beside the road
in a heap of dust, calling piteously for his mother.

"We will get help," promised Winnie. "Stay where
you are, Jamie."

Pressing on towards the bridge, a raggedly-
dressed little girl – alike sore of face, displaying
immense bulb blisters upon her neck and exposed
podgy arms – crashed through the gap in the hedge
sobbing, thence blindly making her way up the road
dragging a teddy bear. A woman rushed from a
nearby cottage calling out her name repeatedly – an
ambulance went rushing past.

At lunch, more unsettling news emerged. "Your
pal, Lucian Finn, and his brother Crepotomus have

been struck down," said Mother, spooning a large portion of shepherd's pie on Betty's plate. "They were fishing, apparently, now the boys are like human pin cushions, covered in big, bulbous blisters, faces red from an agonising rash – but the doctor told Mrs Finn more children, Peter Barnes and Simon Kelpie, have been rushed to the general hospital in Wellingford."

'The shift of vegetation. A mass of plant life on the march', thought Betty, about to open her mouth, but thinking better. Back on the hill with that panoramic view over Glim Glumswick – were her eyes playing tricks? Did this white circle of vegetation shift or not? Her meanderings got interrupted.

"Oh, that really is the end," fumed Mother, stood by the window peering out at the back garden. She and Aunt Medley enjoyed so much pottering about doing the weeding, planting the beds and borders.

"What's the end?"

"I don't recall *that* growing along by the fence."

"Up by the rhododendrons?" queried Aunt Medley.

"Giant hogweed," said Mother, bringing in the gravy boat.

Aunt Medley was emphatic. "A job for Mr Willis, he'll need to uproot the entire plant. How many thousands of seeds does one plant produce?"

Betty's eyes widened as she took in the spiky purple stalks, over twenty feet tall, towering over the borders, she recognised the vast umbrella of white flowers similar to cow parsley. This

invasive species, wishing to impose its will, its presence over the garden.

Lunch over, Betty was tempted to go out into the garden to sunbathe, just to read a book, it was so hot anyhow. Then she realised if she didn't want to end up stung by a surprise visit of a giant hogweed on the move across the lawn, advancing from out of the shrubbery, she'd better act. For starters, she visited the section of river Lucian and his brother Crepotomus invariably fished. Clumps of giant hogweed thrived, seductive bunches of white flowers, the plants – stooping low to be lightly brushed against.

Next, she toured the wheat field where the pair of distressed children were last seen. Along the length of a drainage ditch, giant hogweed, vying to usurp the hedgerow trees.

From each location, Nightingales' Nurseries with its familiar complex of out buildings and main barn that grew and sold many varieties of plants could be easily viewed across the fields.

She hurried round to Professor Lallingtons thatched, half-timbered cottage in Old Pasture Lane. Mrs Hurdlestone, his devoted housekeeper, showed the girl into his crammed study. He was presently stooped over old maps of the county with his magnifying lens, absorbed in the matter of field boundaries during Tudor times. Smoking his gargoyle pipe, he barely glanced up.

"Well, young lady," he puffed. "What can I do for you? 'The Foiled Hamleys Robbery' was surely one of your best yet."

"Tell me about giant hogweed."

The professor grew very serious, leaning back in his chair.

"Not your lesser, common hogweed, of course," said he, tapping the amber stem of his pipe repeatedly. "If one were to cultivate such a horrifying plant, and I say *if*, Betty, you are dicing with your very own life. Originally found in southern Russia, they were wrongly introduced into this country as an ornamental plant, but it was only the tragic death of the renowned plant collectors and horticulturists, Sir Evans and Lord Cryton, that caused the law to be considered banning them. Both worthies killed mysteriously, being strangled and stung to death at their homes. In both instances, a breach of plant cages occurred. I grant, special collections for scientific study exist in the country. But I say, professionals will insist on secure cages as the norm. Any botanist must take due care to ensure safety for the plants can become 'over affectionate' towards the grower," the professor related soberly. "An acquaintance of mine at University College Hospital, I recall, wrote only recently a paper emphasising the extreme danger and toxicity of the giant hogweed. The plant can blind, the hairy stalks contain a vile sap, the skin upon contact burns, the agony unrelenting. Why do you ask, my dear? I trust you are not considering planting one up in your play garden."

"Unfortunately, one is already well rooted," Miss Zmunx replied. "Mother noticed it at lunchtime, but nobody has the faintest clue how it came to be there."

Lallington refilled his pipe and, listening keenly as Betty related her experience atop of the hill that afternoon, at length he responded, "Is this an invasion, are we being surrounded, attacked by a particularly virulent strain – I wonder. My dear Betty how astute of you to implicate Nightingale Nurseries – NIGHTINGALE NURSERIES, the firm also sell shrubs, trees, and roses as well as engaging in landscaping work. An Amos Baggeson organises the growing of stock – propagates trees and shrubs himself. If it transpires to be a lapse on the part of one of the plantsmen ha, I say Blightingale or Frighteningale nurseries more appropriate in our present predicament."

* * *

Churchyards – how many creepy tales and dreadful stories had been written about them. But it wasn't dark, it was sunny and bright as could be.

Betty taking a short cut, walking in silence through the graves a strange thing occurred a little way from the public waste bin. About to pass the well-tended plot of the late Mrs Creech with its green marble chips and vase full of wild daisies – her heart jumped. The tablet was, incredibly, assembling a message, incised letters jumbling about on the headstone and mixing it up – forming new words, new sentences. She rushed over and knelt down, carefully reading the smooth, polished face of the monument.

My dear, so much rumble,

recent rooting activity in our

beautiful churchyard. An alien plant

race, poisonous, set to wreak havoc.

ACT NOW

Regards,

Mrs Eunice Creech (deceased)

Back home, expectant of a magnificent tea, the strawberry cream sponge and scones in particular – accepting a glass of iced lemonade proffered by the domestic, Mrs Appleton, Betty borrowed Aunt Medley's newspaper and hurried upstairs. Browsing the front page of the *Glim Glumswick Echo*, the news proved informative.

'The presence of giant hogweed previously unknown to the county, victims mount – eight at the

*last count, certain requiring to be hospitalised due to
the severity of the burns.'*

GARDENERS BACKLASH

*Facing hours of unremitting toil, digging out the
invaders, risking severe burns, bulb blisters,
poisoned lungs, even blindness, gardeners in the
village are united in demanding the parish council
instigate an epic scale destruction of the giant
hogweed. Alas, there has been few volunteers so far.*

Betty considered the problem. "There is only one person in the whole wide world, I mean machine, that can tackle this outbreak." She sounded determined, stood before the full- length mirror. "Oh please, let it be so."

"Darling," called up her mother, "tea's ready. Oh, and your police steam man is standing outside by the garden gate smoking away. He just turned up."

"P.S.M.!" Betty cried joyfully, clumping down the stairs in her loose sandals. So it was true, it must be her dearest metal friend could communicate. He was not merely a hulk of old iron. Police Steam Man really should have been redundant, gathering rust but instead, Betty went to Leaf Lane with him and was allowed to borrow Mr Clement's little cart which, upon hearing Betty's scheme for clearing the giant hogweed, he hitched onto the metal officer for gathering burnt toxic foliage.

True – P.S.M. was unstoppable, managed to take all the backbreaking work out of destroying batches of giant hogweed, that due to the immense heat radiating from his metal casing lots of the awful plants withered away in close proximity.

Others were wrenched by the stalks, pulling them out by their infernal roots before being hurled in the rear of the cart. For tougher configuration, P.S.M. chucked lumps of red-hot coal from his clip-on fire basket into the plant mass. It was many weeks before so-called fires around the village were finally extinguished.

P.C. Johns and Inspector Haddock, upon being notified, totally approved of the proposed wholesale destruction of the toxic invader. Why, the village constable's first task was to alert the mobile support unit so that the steam man might have plenty of coal and water to fulfil his epic duties. Every effort was maintained to prevent the fires reaching the forest and dry timber stacks set alight.

Once rusting and neglected, stored behind the shed at the police house, not a halfpence of a chance of work, the metal officer born of the loco shed was now hailed a hero. He, who single-handedly rid the town of the infestation of giant hogweed, praised from every quarter. Gardeners, old and young alike, queued up to offer their thanks, spared back-breaking toil and hideous injury. Reporters from the press forming outside the police house to interview P.C. Johns who had put it upon himself to christen the hero HERBERT STEVENSON, using the surname of the famous inventor of 'the rocket' a fine, early locomotive.

Glim Glumswick local council organised a celebr-atory summer procession for the end of the month. The weather proved sunny and gorgeous, the parade

a modest one went ahead. The steam man, garlanded with flowers, the wagonette he stood in for the duration, hauled by a pair of shires. Zmunxy, Lucian, Winnie and Larna Amberly, allowed to join the work team, the inventors Mr Nincombe Poopson, Bunbury and Gilbert atop of the bunting-draped wagon.

Herbert was on everyone's lips, as the crowd cheered and clapped along the route, one end of the High Street to the other. The High Street, not so long ago, a place of ridicule and malfunction, now unstoppable glory. The metal patrolman, smoke puffing from his chimney helmet, waved his only usable arm, his casing smothered in scratches and much scorch burned after encountering the virulent giant hogweed which sought to smother out the town, erase it from the map.

Nothing was ever said, Nightingale Nurseries

never owned up – but it was they Betty felt sure, were culpable for the spread of deadly marching giant hogweed in the village that summer.

CHAPTER

8

Amy Townsley

A sheaf of daffodils embraced in her arms, the pretty, petite, blonde woman, a popular and appealing resident of Glim Glumswick village, a respected artist who painted in oils to great acclaim, being exhibited at the Royal Academy when only sixteen, whose pictures sold at Bond Street galleries and in Europe and America, headed along the flagstone path toward her garden gate, one of her five sprightly cats jealously in tow.

"Why, Betty. Zmunxy! How are you?"

"Very well, thank you, Miss Townsley. Mother wanted you to have these jars of crab apple jelly; me and Lizzie picked the crab apples, actually."

"How very kind. Do come in. I must just place these daffodils in water. Betty, I hear you are rather good at solving mysteries. You have a knack at getting to the crux of a problem. I wish I did, I really do. You see, I think I'm being poisoned; in fact I'm sure of it. My maid Laura is out at present and that's a good thing. Your timing couldn't be better."

"Laura's a jolly super girl, isn't she; the elder sis of my best friend Lizzie Meredith."

"Super? Oh, I'm not so sure. *Underhand*, resentful, more like, cunningly disposed. I may yet have to get rid of her."

"We cannot be talking about the same person, Miss Townsley," Betty exclaimed. "Laura is a most kind-hearted soul, of an exemplary character."

The girl eyed the bunch of yellow blooms gathered in the sink, unbelieving of what she had just heard. Amy Townsley seemed, to her, unusually flustered, pale of feature, her right hand sometimes partly concealed beneath the cuff of her mutton chop blouse. A second friendly cat appeared and then a third, and then a fourth.

"Perhaps something in my food; I can't as yet pin it down, but my maid Laura is a sly one alright. Her shifty glances, her way of trying to over ingratiate herself to me of late. Pointers, you see. I'm quite certain. Perhaps I'd better contact the police."

"Oh no, Miss Townsley!" gasped Betty, horrified by the idea. "You must be mistaken. Laura Meredith is a lovely person."

"You seem most assured of her character, but are you willing to help me, Betty Zmunx? Give practical assistance?"

The girl nodded.

"You know, these beloved, darling cats of mine seem to sense my predicament; Leonard, Sam, Alfred, Harry, Tolly all know something's going on, that I may be being ... oh, I'm so dreadfully bothered, forgive me, this is all so grown-up, Betty."

"Aren't they such pretty, dinky leather collars your cats wear, each with a dainty gold disc bearing an engraved initial," said Betty.

"Yes, they are rather 'dinky', aren't they? Now,

come over here and I'll show you my latest painting. The last time you were at my cottage it was only a pencil sketch."

Miss Townsley settled at her easel, her five adorable cats crouched upon the windowsill and her desk. Removing a cover was revealed a 'fairie folk extravaganza' in oils: maidens wearing toadstool hats, attentive goblins, wood nymphs, all very colourful and pleasing to the eye. Betty thought it grand.

Surrounded by her artist's clutter, creative Amy became a different, more assured person, and yet when she mixed a splodge of oil paint on her palette or attempted to demonstrate a brush stroke, she did find it difficult, her right hand trembled so.

Zmunxy, acutely observant, noted this as significant.

"Well, she may be single, dear," explained Mother at teatime, "but Amy Townsley can't remotely be cast in the same light as those old pussies, old village maids like Miss Grouch and Miss Biers – hysterical spinsters, mean old gossips. She is young, vivacious and pretty with plenty of admirers, which makes what you have told us all the more absurd, so unlike her. *Poisoned*, you say? Well, I never did." Mrs Zmunx helped herself to another delicious muffin dripping with farm butter, whilst her daughter munched on hers. "I mean, we all know Laura is a perfectly delightful girl."

"Could Miss Townsley be a witch? Not the haggy sort, of course," Betty was curious to learn.

"A witch!" Sat opposite round the table, Aunt Medley shook her head doubtfully. "What prompted such an allegation? Are you wishing to inform on our attractive neighbourhood artist? Explain your argument, Betty." She leaned over, cutting herself a slice of damson cake.

"Miss Townsley dotes on her five cats. *Five,*

Auntie, and black cats are long associated with being
..."

"Her familiars, you infer? Quite a record. How on earth does she manage to line them all up on her broomstick, I wonder, when she flies to the local meet? Your daft suggestion aside, you mentioned Amy looked pale, her right-hand trembling when she held her brush and palette knife?"

"Yes, she did," replied the girl smartly.

The aunt had once been a ward sister at St George's Hospital in London, knowledgeable on medicinal drugs, people accidentally poisoned at home and work. Thus, she was perfectly qualified to enquire: "Any other symptoms, dear? Think."

"The artist gnaws her nails, bites them down to the quick."

"We can thus surmise Miss Townsley may be suffering from an acute morbid anxiety, her depressed spirits affecting her outlook. All this nervous behaviour is recent, for I bumped into her at the greengrocers last week and she seemed alright."

"But, could she have been poisoned, Auntie?" "Certainly, poison, say, ingested over a long period reacting in a person's system would reach a crisis. That right hand worries me, though. Going lame, shaky! A doctor should look at that. I expect she's putting it off, embarrassed, and all the worry is mounting up. Plainly she's going a bit dotty."

"What about Laura Meredith?"

"Laura is innocent of any wrongdoing. It's all in the mind. When are you next visiting Amy Townsley, dear?"

"I promised tomorrow morning. We've simply got to sort this out, Auntie. What if she decides to contact the police? This horrid phobia could get Laura into all sorts of trouble."

"I'll come with you, Betty. No, I absolutely must. I know you're a fiercely independent young sleuthhound who likes to work out puzzles for herself, but even Sherlock had his Dr Watson, so your crossword solver aunt will have to do."

"Now come along with me, Amy," Aunt Medley was at her most insistent, "to visit Dr Abbot. Gather your things; you just can't put this off any longer. Thank goodness my niece Betty is so observant. Dr Abbot will be sure to make an appointment with a specialist who will be able to save the use of your right hand, the one you paint with. We're just in the nick of time to save your career. As I say, I recall a patient on my ward, a Horace Webb of Ealing, an artist who suffered similar."

"I never once realised," admitted the pretty young lady, putting on her fashionable chimney pot hat, her aspect more cheerful than the day before. "Oil based paints often contain lead for certain colours. For years my fingers got paint all over them. Under the nails, you say? So, that's how beastly levels of lead entered my bloodstream. It was awfully decent of you to examine me, Miss Medley, to put my mind at rest. I couldn't face the doctor, kept putting off my appointments although I realised, I was poorly."

"Betty!" ordered her aunt sternly, taking no nonsense, "stay here at Miss Townsley's cottage; we shall be back in about an hour. In Laura's absence do the washing up, tidy the artist's materials and prepare a tray of tea things for our return. Put the kettle on to boil, leaves in a warmed teapot, remember."

"Very well, Auntie," the girl replied, a trifle petulantly. After rinsing the cups, Betty slumped heavily with a pronounced bump in the big, old horsehair-covered armchair over by the fireplace. She distinctly heard something drop onto the carpet, a rustle of paper from beneath the comfy seat. All five friendly black cats for some reason converged, expectantly huddled round the chair, laying on their sides, exposing their furry tummies, stretching their paws underneath the seat, curious to claw at whatever had been loosened from a rent in the stiff upholstery fabric. A fat bundle of letters, as it turned out.

Kneeling down, peering wide-eyed, joining the cats, the girl could not resist the lure of this secret stash of personal letters hidden for a reason.

The coal-black cats purred louder and louder, their tails raised in the air, each cat nuzzling up to Betty. She chose, at random, one of the envelopes from the bundle, opening and examining the letter within. She scanned it but briefly, not wishing to over-pry. It read: 'My dearest, most darling, most adored Amy' and ended, 'All my love, *Tolly Marchmount*.'

Another thus: 'Oh sweetest Muse, my own dearest swan Amy.' The letter ended, 'Love you always,

Leonard Simpkins'. Another concluded: 'Love you, ducks, *Sam* Weldon.'

Sam, Leonard, Tolly: these were surely Christian names attributed to the black cats initialled on the discs — mere coincidence? She thought not. Hurriedly replacing the bundle of love letters back in its niche in the stuffing of the horsehair-covered armchair, keeping her eye on the grandfather clock, she began preparing for her aunt's and Miss Townsley's return, determined to pursue her witch theory, make discreet enquiries in the village.

"Tolly Marchmount, according to Mrs Redfern at the post office, apparently went to sea and was never heard of again. Sam Weldon suddenly signed up to join the empire army to see the world — no word since. Leonard Simpkins left a scribbled note to his mother. He was on a banana boat heading for Buenos Aires. Isn't that a weeny bit suspicious, Mummy, each young man suddenly uprooting, never communicating!"

"Witches on the brain. I know you're being sincere, Betty, but your idea that these young men of the village, her past lovers, have by means of a spell been magically transformed into her familiars, those five cuddly black cats, is preposterous!" insisted Mother, knitting by the hearth. "However, your impudence at reading personal correspondence, love letters addressed to Amy, is really quite reprehensible and you should be put on bread and water for a month, confined to your room!"

"A fine fiction, my dear," said Aunt Medley, glancing up from her *Times* crossword, a glass of sherry at hand, "but in the real world, I am glad to report Miss Townsley's hand is on the mend and her relationship with Laura the maid back to normal – an equilibrium of happiness and laughter restored."

CHAPTER 9

The Crafty Grandma

ven after all this time, Grandma Nibbs was really mad, still fuming, like her equally resentful daughter-in-law, a bitter woman if ever, seeking revenge against the nice fat policeman, P.C. Johns, for arresting, for helping convict Alfie Nibbs, a son and husband. He, a father of nine hateful brats, found guilty by a jury, sentenced to a long spell of imprisonment, breaking rocks at Dartmoor, the bleak moorland surrounding the prison, notorious for damp weather and boggy conditions; not very health inducing or inspiring for someone locked up for years in a narrow, freezing cold, stone-clad cell, fed gruel.

But the real problem came not from the fact Alfie

Nibbs was a convicted housebreaker, a violent crook with a grudge, but the fact his elderly grandmother was a real, bona fide witch who had the ability to cast horrid spells when she chose. Some years back it will be remembered P.C. Johns suffered multiple bicycle punctures doing his rounds of Glim Glumswick village, causing untold grief, punctures occurring for no reason at every turn, mysteriously, one after the other, to both front and rear pneumatic tyres; no one could work out the cause until Betty Zmunx discovered runes, magical symbols scratched onto the inside of his cycle clips. Cunning indeed!

But now, at the beginning of November, P.C. Johns must be on his guard, for a message, a new reason to remain especially vigilant, had been discovered pinned to a street guy on a barrow 'Remember, remember the fifth of November,

"But is the obscure message actually related to the Nibbs family?" pointed out the village constable, taking afternoon tea at the Zmunx's cottage in Old Pasture Lane, sat at table with Mother, Aunt Medley and Betty, who knelt on the tufty rug before the coal fire toasting muffins on a long fork.

"My best friend, Lizzie, who lives opposite the Nibbs, says it's her writing. Oh, what can she be planning?" young Betty Zmunx mused, a frown on her face. The fat policeman seemed unconcerned, chomping on a muffin, dribbling hot butter down his many wobbly chins.

"Mumbo jumbo, hocus-pocus the vicar calls it. I'm not going to let that bothersome woman or her family intimidate me, that's definite. I'm ashamed to say this, Mrs Zmunx, Miss Medley, but I'd like to ring her scrawny neck, or as likely burn Grandma Nibbs at the stake."

Suddenly, the constable lost his voice, gripping his throat. His eyes bulged and he proceeded to go very red in the face which ballooned out. He began to heave and choke; a bit of muffin must have gone down the wrong way, blocking his windpipe. Mother leapt up and slapped him vigorously on the back. Wheezing and spitting crumbs, he eventually recovered enough to eat three more of Mother's delicious, toasted muffins besides, without further discomfort.

"Well, I'll be off," said he. "I've a bag of old togs I left on your back step, Mrs Zmunx; I'll just go and fetch it, just odds and ends, mind, for the up and coming jumble sale. A pair of my old boots, some thrown out clothes, jacket, trousers, cap; someone'll be glad of 'em, I s'pect."

"How kind, how generous," cooed Aunt Medley finishing the last dregs of her cup of tea, smiling charmingly.

"Well, I'll be blowed," P.C. Johns exclaimed, stooping beneath a low oak ceiling beam, re-entering the cottage parlour.

"What is it?" asked Mother clearing things away, indicating by a stern look Betty should help with washing up while Aunt finished her absorbing crossword puzzle.

"The bag of jumble! My bag of jumble has been stolen! Someone, dunno who, must have sneaked up the path by your dustbins and run off. Good luck to 'em, I say." He grinned. "Only old clobber. Remember, remember the fifth of November, gunpowder, treason and plot." He laughed raucously. "That's tonight and I'm on duty. See if I can nab one of those Nibbs children stuffing a lighted banger through a letter box. Happened last year; do you recall that barn fire, the thatch set ablaze by a firework rocket? Good day ladies."

The fat policeman replaced his helmet, remounting his trusty bicycle before waving and setting off from the kerb. Betty Zmunx watched from the latticed window, her heart filled with foreboding, the warning note found pinned to the street guy preying on her mind.

Later, by diligent enquiry while walking her little Scotch terrier, Bertie, the girl discovered Mrs Bunn from next door, remembered seeing one of the Nibbs' rough urchins, Moses, jumping over the garden gate of the Zmunxs' country cottage, fleeing down toward the high street, a cloth bag in his hand.

So, the old clothes belonging to the friendly village constable, P.C. Johns, were serving some nefarious purpose – to do him harm, Betty reflected severely, and this really got her thinking ...

That evening, a constable had to be called in from another village for P.C. Johns lay dangerously ill in bed, the village doctor in attendance. He had gone down with a high fever, was sweating profusely and his bed sheets wringing wet. Mrs Smedwick, a nurse, believed him to be suffering from a bout of malaria, but nothing they tried, no medical procedure would bring down his body temperature. He was, by half past seven, barely conscious, his forehead boiling to the touch.

"P.C. Johns may die at this rate," remarked the doctor despairingly, fearing the worst, unknowing of the actual root cause of the rampant fever that threatened the fat (now rapidly thinning) policeman's very life.

While firework rockets twinkled across the sky and Roman candles popped in gardens and smoke from bonfires drifted across the village, Betty arrived at the Nibbs' run-down cottage with five of her friends, including Lizzie and her sister, all known from the schoolhouse. Each child carried a bucket of slopping water.

Peering over the fence, the children were confronted by the most ghastly, blood-curdling scene imaginable. The appalling grandma, Mrs Nibbs, and her nine unruly offspring NAKED. Pink flesh, white ribs, rolls of sagging skin in abundance, they were dancing anti-clockwise around a pentangle, that is a magical circle, painted in chalky white paint on the grass lawn. Within the pentangle was a roaring bonfire, on top of which was propped a fiery effigy of P.C. Johns, the guy decked out in his old boots, cloth cap and jumble clothes stolen that afternoon. The guy was rapidly being consumed, sparks rising into the sky, the Nibbs clan chanting to the devil.

Zmunxy and her friends clambered over the wall into the ramshackle garden and bravely rushed forward brandishing water buckets to douse the worst of the flames, scattering the naked Nibbs, confusing proceedings.

The next morning, the fat policeman, cheerful and ready to assist, was out and about as usual, although he appeared to have drastically lost weight.

MOTHERHOOD

CHAPTER 19
Tudor Teams Up

*O*ne night, a pair of ghost-rats, Filch and Raker, appeared at the ivy-clad vault, stood for centuries in the grounds of Mulberry Manor. Scrambling onto the masonry step, the pair grew wary.

"This is the place, ain't it?"

"Yeah," said the other, whiskers twitching. "Like old Sir Blunderbust directed. Tudor Sefton."

One of the long - tailed brown rats stood on its haunches.

"Clever gal. Sleuf, I 'ear. Wonder if she 'as one of 'em fairy daemons – bleedin' stoat or weasel, even a monkey – Old Sharkey mentioned." He, a ghostly white rat from Oxfordshire, had told the pair strange, inspiring tales about the city. Daemons were all the rage, apparently.

"Chimps – blow that for a lark. Still, scramble up that ironwork, Raker, and ruddy well scratch yer claws on the ornamental door, see what 'appens, pal."

Suddenly, the vault's entrance gate, grating from rust, ascended like a portcullis and two rodents engulfed in a bright green effusion of light, caught in a whirling forcefield, spun around upwards, upwards and upwards.

"Blimey, lay orf, will yer," squealed Raker breathlessly, reeling from the experience. They both landed squarely in front of a lamp on a stick.

"A dubious duo, a pair of dirty sewer rats," spoke

a pretty girl sat up in her coffin, combing her long dark hair with a brush left her long ago by Betty. She was wearing a nightshirt, or to put it more morbidly, was it a grave shroud? Whatever, it looked most becoming. The coffin hovered a foot or so above a carved plinth. "What are you two doing snooping round my vault, I'd like to know?"

"Dirty – leave orf. 'Onest, I ain't never been near a sewer. We're 'renewed', like yerself, luv," insisted Filch, somewhat aggrieved. The rat had met his own end, his physical self when alive being pecked to death by a pesky seagull after straying onto the bird's breakfast territory round by the manor house bin, found himself a nice bit of crusty ham sandwich too. Raker had suffered terminal indigestion when he stupidly swallowed poison, bait laid down by the then butler up at the big house. Rattus norvegicus in memoriam.

"'Ere," Filch said, nibbling his ethereal claws,

eager to sate his curiosity regarding the musings of that sophisticated white rodent from Oxford. "Scuse me askin', ain't you got no daemons, ain't that the word? What you sort of 'ave on yer shoulder, or summat fancy – ferret, like a pet, so to speak, but attached to yer earthly personality. Me and him could easy do that job if yer want."

"Not me," she laughed gaily. "Another world, I'd wager."

"We ain't sewer."

"I know, I know, but if I did have a daemon, I'd probably settle for a squirrel with a ribboned bell round it's neck, sorry. Now you oafs explain yourselves."

Filch became deadly serious.

"Poltergeists, ma'am," said he gulping, leaning on his long tail. "Lot of bovver up at the big house. Disturbance. I ain't neffer, in all my time dead felt nor heard anyfink like it. We was told maybe you could *help, Tudor. Boaf the livin' an' the dead at the manor is united. We gotta do somefink, and flippin' quickly. 'Whatever', is growing in strength. Gord knows what may happen next. Destruction of our dear old place is unthinkable."*

The same night, Tudor Sefton was contacted, Betty had a very vivid dream, or was it a reality? Somebody at the end of her bed announced herself to be Beatrix Potter. She was stood under a cottage porch, clasping a wide- brimmed, floppy hat. Rosy-cheeked and blue- eyed, she was short and dumpy. Her dress sense practical, country tweeds – her herringbone costume, with thick skirt stretching down to her ankles. On her feet a pair of sturdy clog-like shoes.

"I report to you, Betty, from Hilltop House in the Lake District," said she. Miss Potter was, of course, renowned for her animal tales, the wonderful illustrated books, and Betty still kept a collection that she cherished. *The Tale of Peter Rabbit*, *The Tale of Tiggy Winkle*, and many more. "Betty, my dear, I know you're grown up but you really must look up your old friend Larna Amberley, for she is much perplexed. Do trouble yourself to visit her tomorrow. Leave it no later, and who knows, my little picture books may even help. Goodbye."

Remarkably, this non-scary vision of the Lakeland author, then alive, still writing and drawing, changed with a tremulous shiver into invisibility and vanished. For some reason, Betty dreamed of a past lecture Professor Lallington gave at the village hall, about Glim Glumswick Ley Line and how it was directly beneath Mulberry Manor. Betty was awoken by the sound of birds twittering and her baby crying – dawn peeping through the curtains. She threw back the bedclothes to attend her youngest infant. Meanwhile, her son Timothy, a bright boy of seven, was stirring in the next room and presently came in to see his mother. It was six o'clock.

After breakfast, Betty was determined to contact her old childhood friend, Larna Amberley, who herself was married and had kids of her own, and was still living at the old manor house. Baby happily chortling in her pram, Timothy clutching mother's coat sleeve, Betty Cosgrove, for that was her married name, now in her twenties, wed to an officer, Bill Cosgrove, in the Royal Navy, presently serving abroad, due back at Portsmouth at the end of the month, set off for the bus.

Larna Amberley was delighted to see her friend of yesteryear, and what a lot of catching up they had to do. The fun memories of that holiday spent in exciting circumstances, when Betty, together with the ghost sleuth, Tudor Sefton, in her flying coffin, cracked the case of the The Old Violin so effectively. A number of staff, taken into police custody as a consequence of a valuable stolen violin.

"Funny you should turn up like this. I was about to write you a letter, Betty. We've got a problem – a big one – at Mulberry Manor. You're sort of my last resort. My husband, Freddy, is of course at work – I'd have loved to introduce you."

"The local bank manager from the branch along the High Street?"

"That's him. Anyhow, we – including my girls, Penny and Pat – are becoming increasingly alarmed, if that's the correct word. More like scared, actually."

"What about?"

"Last couple of nights, around midnight, a sort of loud chattering mist rushes through the house knocking over suits of armour, crashing down portraits, shifting ornaments, blowing out the fires in our rooms, even the chandeliers rattle for a time. Last year, we had a surveyor's report, everything is structurally sound – the buildings in good nick."

"Well, I must say Larna this house mist seems decidedly weird."

The baby started gurgling, wiggling her legs and podgy arms about, allowing Betty to pass her infant onto Larna's lap to dote over. Their other children, the girls and Timothy, were up in the play room racing shiny-printed tin toy cars against the skirting board.

A vase, quite unexpectedly, slithered quietly to the edge of the ornate mantelpiece and came to rest. The ormolu clock prettily struck thirteen chimes.

"Tudor, the spirit sleuth's with us," mentioned Betty. "She must know something." She felt that familiar thrill of a united team. How this married woman yearned to recapture those childhood adventures once more. Goodness, then she remembered the Glumswick LEY LINE, the conduit of magical energy running beneath the manor.

That night abed, at her beloved Old Pasture cottage, inherited from Mother, sleep proved elusive. She kept wondering what this 'chattering mist' must mean. At some stage, she was alerted by a loud, distinct tapping at the window. The young woman was seized by an old excitement. Hurrying over to the sill, she could hardly wait to part the floral-patterned curtains.

A never-forgotten pale girl, wearing a Tudor box hood, lined with pearls and a velvet dress with a high collar denoting, in those far-off days, wealth and privilege, lovingly appraised her friend from modern times through the glass. Her sharply angular face lit by the glowing lantern projected on a stick from her flying nail- studded coffin, then in hover mode, many feet above the cottage garden – the paved path and flowerbeds looked an awful long way down.

Recalling her tuition, Betty did not lack enthusiasm, nor did she hesitate, but she was a grown woman now, the mother of two children. Stepping up onto her holiday trunk, she tried every way to squeeze herself through the open window, ending up like a contortionist, but it never worked. Two brown rats poked their bewhiskered heads up.

"I'm not sure," she faltered, "whether I should even be doing this, Tudor- baby's sleeping in the cot, Timothy's in the next room."

"No need," said the ghost girl confidently, putting her at ease. "Dearest Betty, you know about the chattering house mist – you must visit Larna again. Here's what the problem is and how to solve it."

***

"Larna, might you recall a fire when you were little, a blaze that look hold. Must have been traumatic at the time. You'd likely want to forget. Shove it to the back of your weeny mind."

Sun pouring in from the lattice windows, the women were enjoying a cup of tea in the oak-panelled drawing room of the historic old house. The new arrival, baby Molly, taking much of their attention.

"Can't say I do. Like what? Like part of the Manor going up in flames? Thatch, kitchen fire, chimney stack? No, nothing dramatic that I can think of Betty."

"Boo, hee, hee, boo, hee, hee." The infant wriggled about laughing merrily.

"A hutch fire!"

Bouncing the baby on her knee, Larna thought for a bit, then finally something dawned.

"Oh," she gasped. "You've brought it all back. I remember now. How we treasure tiny animals like people at that age, and how quickly we forget so much wisdom. My poor hamster, my gerbils, my adorable mice and rabbits kept round by the kitchen garden. I recall there was a lad," Larna frowned, "an apprentice gardener, who one evening tripped over a length of hosepipe on the path dropping his lamp. The glass shattered spilling oil, the flames fanned by a breeze and the wooden hutches all went up in smoke. When I got there, everything was ashes. I cried and cried, but it was definitely only an accident. No blame apportioned, I got a puppy out of it anyhow, one of those things, I 'spose."

Now comes the crux of the mystery, however daft it might sound.

"What if I told you this chattering mist, the psychic cloud that rushes through your rooms knocking stuff over is composed of those same animals, only their ghostly forms scampering as fast as can be around your house. So fast, in fact, they are a blur creating mischief, cos they feel long neglected. Would you believe it?"

"Not really. Well, I might, but my husband would only laugh. Freddy is a practical sort."

"So am I," Betty retorted. "So is Tudor Sefton, who sussed it all out." At that moment, a candlestick shifted off the mantelpiece and nodded in mid-air before returning. "Now, what you'd better do is this, and Tudor agrees – get your girls, like a school project, to build hutches on the same spot, the site of the fire, then populate them with hamsters, gerbils, mice and rabbits got from the pet shop. You see where this is leading."

"I do, my girls can clean out the hutches, do the lettuces, the fresh straw, water bowls – all coming back to me. Order sacks of feed. Oh, Betty, they'll simply adore looking after the animals. What a grand idea."

"And then, the little ghosts would have company."

"Of course ..."

The Fairytale Detective Series

Halloweenland

Betty's Chronicles of Glim Glumswick

Betty – more of the Fairytale Detective

www.ingramcontent.com/pod-product-compliance
Lightning Source LLC
Chambersburg PA
CBHW061217210726
48294CB00006B/1874